ISBN 0-86163-398-9

Text and illustrations copyright © 1990
Award Publications Limited

First published 1990

Published by Award Publications Limited,
Spring House, Spring Place,
Kentish Town, London NW5 3BH

Printed in Belgium

THE LITTLE BLUE TRAIN

by Hayden McAllister

illustrated by Alan Fredman

Award Publications - London

The New Railway

Deep in the heart of Fir Tree Forest there was great excitement.
The little blue engine was having a bath.

Rabbits were fetching buckets of water from the river. Boris
Badger was splashing soapy water over the blue boiler with a
large mop. Sid Squirrel was perched on top of the little blue
engine, polishing the funnel with a duster. Fred Mouse was
cleaning the wheels with a brush. And Tony Tortoise was
rubbing hard at the brass rail on the side of the boiler, trying to
make it shine like gold.

But where was Bob the engine driver?

Bob was in his log cabin. He was taking a bath too! He wanted to look his best for he knew that today was a very special day in the life of the little blue train.

It was also a special day for all the animals of Fir Tree Forest…

A new railway line had been built right across Goose Lake. It was to be opened by Mayor Boris Bear and everyone wanted to be there to see the official opening ceremony.

Bob was very excited because he'd never driven the little blue train across a lake before.

Just before one o'clock, a very clean-looking little blue train stood in Fir Tree Station.
There were so many passengers to pick up; rabbits, badgers, squirrels, tortoises, mice, and even a pigeon who perched on top of one of the carriages.

The little blue train was greatly looking forward to this special journey. His clean blue boiler was as bright as the blue sky. Coloured ribbons were tied to his engine, and he had a big smile on his face.

Bob the engine driver wore his best uniform and looked very smart indeed. He checked his pocket watch, and when it was exactly one o'clock he sounded the little blue engine's whistle: 'Wheep-wheep!'

Everyone cheered as the little blue engine slowly began to puff its way out of Fir Tree Station.

Porgy Pig, who had overslept, came rushing into the station squealing, 'Wait for me! Wait for me!' He just managed to get on the train in time!

Moments later, they were all on their way to the grand opening of the Goose Lake Railway.

The little blue train was speeding happily along through Fir Tree Forest. Bob was whistling to himself. The pigeon was asleep on the carriage roof and the passengers were eating their various sandwiches. These included everything from carrot and lettuce sandwiches for the rabbits to fried banana for Porgy Pig.

Suddenly Bob saw a great red blob on the track ahead. As quick as a flash he pulled the brake lever. The little blue train screeched to a halt.

Porgy Pig almost choked on his sandwich and the passengers nearly fell out of their seats with fright.

Bob climbed down from his cab and scratched his head in puzzlement. Then he realised that the big red blob was really a hot-air balloon and basket.

The little blue engine had never seen a hot-air balloon before and looked very surprised.

Bob walked towards the air balloon. As he did so, Maurice Mole, wearing his flying goggles, appeared out of the trees.

'Oh, I'm so glad you managed to stop!' gasped Maurice. 'My balloon ran out of hot air and I landed on the track with quite a bump!'

'I'm glad we managed to stop too,' replied Bob. 'Otherwise we might have burst your nice red balloon!'

'I was hoping to watch the grand opening of the Goose Lake Railway from the air,' explained Maurice Mole.

'Well perhaps I could get the little blue engine to puff some more hot air into your balloon,' suggested Bob.

'That would be marvellous!' cried Maurice.

Bob and Maurice fixed the balloon over the funnel of the little blue engine. Two strong rabbits held on to the basket while the little blue engine puffed hard into the balloon.

When the balloon was full, Maurice climbed into the basket and Bob called, 'Hold on tight!'

The rabbits let go of the basket and the hot-air balloon rose into the sky.

Maurice Mole waved at the passengers below and called, 'Thank you very much!' to Bob and the little blue engine.

'We'll see you at the grand opening of the Goose Lake Railway!' shouted Bob.

Bob waited a few minutes until the little blue engine had got it's breath back. Then he climbed back into the cab.

Soon the little blue engine was steaming down the track once more towards Goose Lake.

At three o'clock the little blue train was rushing down a long steep track and into the valley where Goose Lake lay.

As they chugged round the final bend they saw Bertha Bluebird. She waved to them from above a green signal lantern in a tall tree. The little blue engine gave her a friendly whistle and Bob gave her a big smile and a wave.

'We're nearly there!' cried Bob.

'Wheep-wheep!' went the little blue engine.

Boris Bear the Mayor, was
already waiting for them at the
edge of the lake. He looked very important indeed in his green
waistcoat and top hat.

Lots of animals had come to see the opening of the new
railway. When they had all settled down, the Mayor spoke
through a loud hailer. 'Welcome to Goose Lake Railway,' he
boomed in a *very* loud voice. 'I declare this railway *officially*
open!'

Then, with a pair of scissors, he cut the bright yellow ribbon
which was tied across the shiny new track of the Goose Lake
Railway. Everyone cheered.

The local geese honked happily. Everyone on the shore waved at the passengers. The pigeon started to coo, and two little squirrels in a boat rowed along beside the train.

When he was halfway across the lake the little blue engine spotted his old friend the little yellow engine on the far side. He gave a friendly whistle and the yellow engine tooted back. Next time they met, they would have something really exciting to talk about. In fact, the opening of the Goose Lake Railway was something that everyone would remember for a very long time.

The little blue engine sounded its whistle excitedly. Bob took off the brake and the little blue train slowly rolled on to the track above the water. Everyone held their breath.

'I hope nothing nasty happens,' squealed Porgy Pig, 'because I don't think the little blue engine can swim! Come to think of it – neither can I!' But the little blue train moved smoothly out across Goose Lake.

Looking up, Bob saw Maurice Mole flying high above them. He was waving to everyone below. 'Don't fall out!' cried Bob.

The Lonely Snowman

Bob the engine driver was lying in
bed in his log cabin…

It was dark outside for it was
almost midnight. Stars could be seen
peeping between the tops of the big
fir trees. A cold wind was blowing
and making strange whistling noises
in the trees. It reminded Bob of the
noise the little blue engine made
when he sounded the whistle. In fact the sound was so like the
whistle of the little blue train that Bob got out of bed and lit the
lantern. He put on his wellington boots and coat.

Then, still carrying the lantern, he went outside to see if the
little blue train was still asleep in its shed.

Once outside, Bob noticed that the railway-shed door was wide open. He could see a red glow brightening the darkness.

'That's very strange,' thought Bob as he drew nearer to the shed. 'I hope the little blue train is all right.'

When Bob got to the door he could see the little blue engine standing there as usual. The odd thing was that someone had opened the fire-box door – he could see the glow inside the cab.

A moment later, Bob saw a rabbit and a pig warming themselves in the heat given out by the little blue engine's fire.

'It's Pip Rabbit and Porgy Pig!' gasped Bob. 'What on earth are you doing here at this time of night?'

'We're sorry to have disturbed you, Bob,' said Pip Rabbit, 'but we're worried.'

'Yes, cold and worried,' squealed Porgy Pig.

'Then tell me what's wrong,' suggested Bob.

'Well!' said Pip Rabbit. 'Yesterday, Bertha Bluebird said she saw a man in a white suit and a bowler hat standing alone in Fir Tree Forest.'

'What's wrong with that?' asked Bob.

'Nothing,' said Porgy Pig. 'But Bertha said that he looked so sad and lonely.'

'I'll tell you what we'll do,' said Bob. 'We'll all go out in the little blue train at sunrise tomorrow and search for him.'

Next morning, the sun was just climbing out of bed when the little blue train pulled into Fir Tree Station.

Pip Rabbit and Porgy Pig came rushing along the platform to greet Bob. They were wearing woollen hats and scarves because it was so cold.

The little blue engine, who had hardly had a wink of sleep all night, gave a great big yawn.

'I think we'd better be on our way,' said Bob, laughing. 'Otherwise the little blue engine might fall asleep!'

As they set off, a few flakes of snow began to fall…

Once they were on their way Bob said, 'First we need to find Bertha Bluebird. She should be able to tell us where to find the lonely man in the white suit. Do either of you know where Bertha will be at this time of day?' he asked Pip and Porgy.

'She usually sings in the dawn chorus in the trees beside the old signal-box,' said Pip.

'That will please the little blue engine,' said Bob, smiling. 'He loves to listen to the birds singing.'

'Wheep-wheep!' whistled the little blue engine.

When they reached the old signal-box Bob stopped the train. He could see Bertha perched on top of the old signal-box roof with three friendly robins. All the birds wore woollen hats and mufflers because it was so chilly.

'Hello!' chirped Bertha Bluebird.

'Hello, Bertha!' said Bob. 'We've come to ask you about the lonely man in the white suit and bowler hat.'

'Oh, yes,' said Bertha. 'The sad man. He's in the valley at the foot of the mountains. If you follow me I'll take you to him.'

Bertha Bluebird flew along the railway track. The three robins flew behind her. Then came the little blue train with Bob, Porgy and Pip on board.

As they approached the valley at the foot of the mountains they saw some patches of snow lying on the ground. The birds with their bright feathers, and the little blue train, made a colourful sight against the snow.

A mountain bear smiled and waved to them as the train passed by.

'That big bear looks nice and warm in his fur coat,' said Porgy Pig.

When they reached the valley, Bertha Bluebird and the three robins flew off into the forest. Bob stopped the little blue train and the three friends got out. Then Bob, Porgy and Pip followed the birds into the forest.

In the far distance they could see the snowy peaks of the mountains…

They had walked a long way before Bertha Bluebird and the robins came rushing back towards them.

'The sad man in the bowler hat has gone!' cried Bertha anxiously.

'Are you sure?' said Bob. 'Shouldn't we search a little while longer?'

'It's no use,' said Bertha. 'The local sparrows say that he has completely disappeared.'

'Oh dear, what a shame!' exclaimed Bob. 'It looks as though our journey has been wasted.'

'Humph! Now we'll have to plod all the way back to the little blue train,' moaned Porgy Pig. 'And my little piggy toes are almost frozen.'

When the three friends returned to the edge of the forest they found a surprise waiting for them. The man in the black bowler hat and the white suit was standing right beside the little blue engine!'

'He's a snowman!' gasped Pip Rabbit. 'He must have come down from the mountains.'

'Well, hello!' boomed the snowman.

'What are you doing down here?' asked Pip Rabbit.

'I'm here,' replied the snowman, 'because it's – BRRrr – too cold for me on the mountain top! Snowman Village is all very well – but it's so chilly up there! Mind you,' he admitted, 'I'm lonely down here all by myself.'

'Why not come back with us?' suggested Porgy Pig.

'Yes,' agreed Bob, as he smiled at the snowman. 'Travel back with us on the little blue train.'

'Oh! May I?' asked the snowman, delighted with the idea.

'I've never been on a railway train before,' he admitted, climbing on board.

'If you hold on tight,' advised Bob. 'You will be quite safe.' Bertha Bluebird and the three robins perched beside the snowman to keep him company. Soon the little blue engine was steaming back towards Fir Tree Station. They were travelling so fast that the snowman had to hold onto his bowler hat.

'This is great fun!' he cried. 'It's even better than sledging in the snow.'

'Wheep-wheep,' whistled the little blue engine.

The animals of Fir Tree Forest could not believe their eyes as they saw the little blue train pass by.

'The little blue train is carrying a snowman!' they cried. The snowman liked it so much in Fir Tree Forest that he now returns every winter to work at Fir Tree Station.

There he collects the tickets and sweeps the platform. And when the little blue train is about to leave the station he cries: 'All aboard!' and raises his snowman's hat. Then the little blue engine goes 'Wheep-wheep!' and gives him a great big smile.